13.95

DUE

this
·little·barron's·
book belongs to

....

....

First edition for the United States and Canada published 1999 by
Barron's Educational Series, Inc.

Copyright © Nicola Smee 1997

First published in Great Britain by Orchard Books in 1997.

All inquiries should be addressed to:
Barron's Educational Series, Inc.
250 Wireless Boulevard, Hauppauge, New York 11788
http://www.barronseduc.com

Library of Congress Catalog Card No.: 98-74975
International Standard Book No. 0-7641-0866-2

Printed in Italy

9 8 7 6 5 4 3 2 1

Freddie Visits
the Doctor

Nicola Smee

· little · barron's ·

I've got a sore throat
and so has Bear.
Mom's taking us to
see the doctor.

"Open wide
and say, Aaah!"
says Doctor.

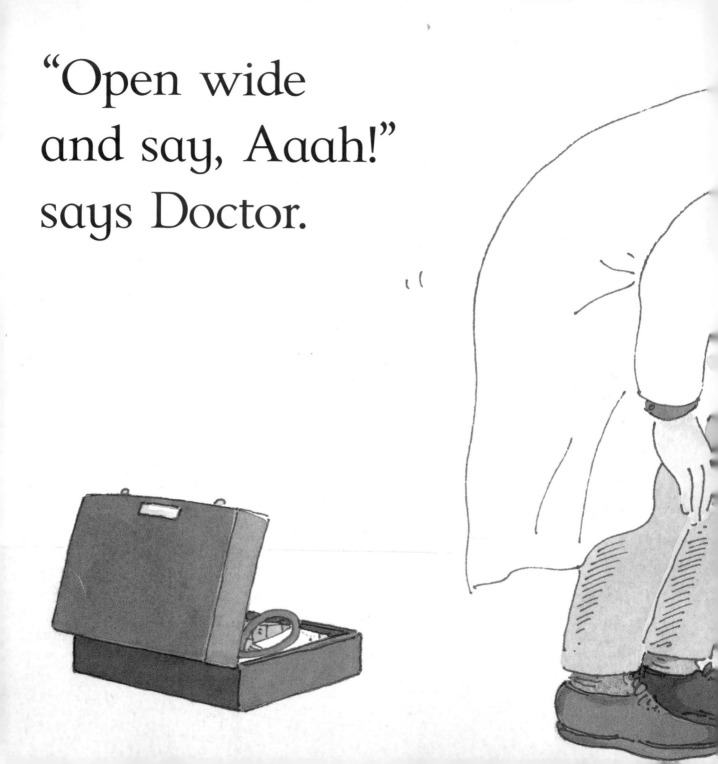

He looks into
our ears with
a little light.

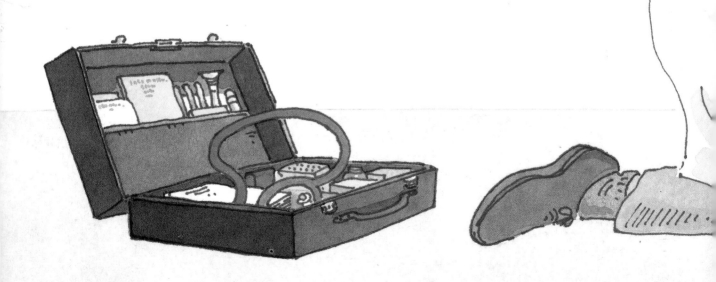

"Take a deep breath," says Doctor, and he listens to our chests with his stethoscope.

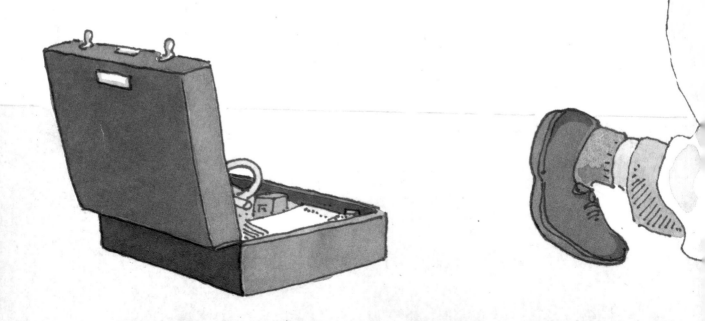

"Bear's fine, but this medicine will soon make you better, Freddie," says Doctor.

"Here you are, Freddie," says the pharmacist.

"Time for your medicine," says Mom. "You'll soon be well again."

Mmmm, that's nice!
My throat feels
better already.

What's a FISH ?
¿Qué es un PEZ ?

Anna Kaspar
Traducción al español:
Eduardo Alamán

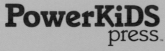

PowerKiDS
press
New York

Published in 2013 by The Rosen Publishing Group, Inc.
29 East 21st Street, New York, NY 10010

First Edition

Editor: Amelie von Zumbusch   Traducción al español: Eduardo Alamán
Book Design: Ashley Drago

Photo Credits: Cover © www.iStockphoto.com/Luís Fernando Curci Chavier; p. 5 Paul Souders/ Getty Images; pp. 6, 16 Shutterstock.com; p. 9 © www.iStockphoto.com/Nancy Nehring; pp. 10–11 © www.iStockphoto.com/Rainer von Brandis; p. 12 Medioimages/Photodisc/ Thinkstock; p. 15 © www.iStockphoto.com/Roman Sigaev; p. 19 iStockphoto/Thinkstock; p. 20 Werner Van Steen/Getty Images; p. 23 www.iStockphoto.com/Darren Pearson.

Library of Congress Cataloging-in-Publication Data

Kaspar, Anna.
[What's a fish? Spanish & English]
What's a fish? = ¿Qué es un pez? / by Anna Kaspar. — 1st ed.
    p. cm. — (All about animals = Todo sobre los animales)
Includes index.
ISBN 978-1-4488-6701-1 (library binding)
1. Fishes—Juvenile literature. I. Title. II. Title: Qué es un pez?
QL617.2.K3718 2013
597—dc23
                                        2011023756

Web Sites: Due to the changing nature of Internet links, PowerKids Press has developed an online list of Web sites related to the subject of this book. This site is updated regularly. Please use this link to access the list:
www.powerkidslinks.com/aaa/fish/

Manufactured in the United States of America

CPSIA Compliance Information: Batch #CS12PK: For Further Information contact Rosen Publishing, New York, New York at 1-800-237-9932

Contents / Contenido

✳ ✳ ✳ ✳ ✳ ✳ ✳ ✳ ✳ ✳ ✳ ✳

Fish are a type of animal. Most fish have **fins**.

Los peces son una clase de animal. La mayoría de los peces tiene **aletas**.

4

6

All fish live in water. Fish are covered in **scales**.

Todos los peces viven en el agua. Los peces están cubiertos de **escamas**.

Fish have **gills**. They use their gills to breathe.

La mayoría de los peces tienen **branquias**. Las branquias se usan para respirar.

Some kinds of fish swim in big groups. These are called **schools**.

Algunas clases de peces nadan en grandes grupos. A estos grupos se les llama **bancos**.

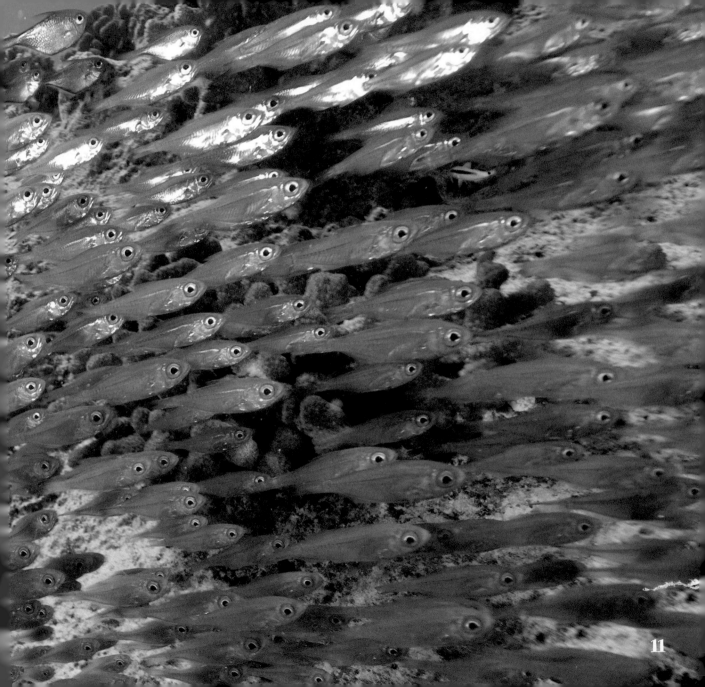

Longsnout sea horses live in the Atlantic Ocean. Ocean water is salty.

Los caballitos de mar viven en el Océano Atlántico. El agua del océano es salada.

Carp live in freshwater. This is water that is not salty.

Las carpas viven en agua dulce.

15

Piranhas live in South American rivers. They are known for their sharp teeth.

Las pirañas viven en los ríos de Sudamérica. Las pirañas son famosas por sus filosos dientes.

Lionfish are poisonous. Their colors scare off animals that want to eat them.

El pez león es venenoso. El pez león tiene colores que espantan a los otros animales que lo quieren atacar.

Great white sharks are hunters.
They find their food by its smell.

Los tiburones blancos son
cazadores. Los tiburones
blancos encuentran su
comida por el olor.

21

Sailfish often jump out of the water. They are the world's fastest fish.

Con frecuencia el pez vela salta fuera del agua. El pez vela es el pez más rápido del mundo.

WORDS TO KNOW/
PALABRAS QUE DEBES SABER

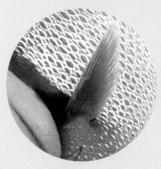

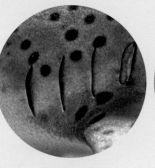

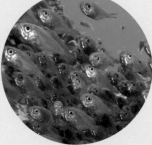

fin/
(la) aleta

gills/
(las) branquias

scales/
(las) escamas

school/
(el) banco

INDEX

ÍNDICE